The Lost Lyrics

of

Schaeffer Cox

Francis August Schaeffer Cox

The Lost Lyrics of Schaeffer Cox

Contributors:	Angela Clemons
	Elizabeth Sarver
	David Triemert
Cover Design:	David Andrew Ingram, MagneticFlux Design

Permissions

Schaeffer's Angels
14526 Piney Road
Mulberry, AR 72947

ISBN: 978-0-9995481-0-3 (softcover)

ISBN: 978-0-9995481-1-0 (ebook)

Printed in the United States of America.

Dedication

This book is dedicated to anyone who sings

these lyrics to life,

for in doing so you will have helped

a tiny part of me

escape this 7' x 9' cell,

where I have lived all these years.

About the Author

Schaeffer Cox in prison

Francis August Schaeffer Cox, aka Schaeffer, is a political prisoner who is being held in the Communication Management Unit (CMU) in Terre Haute, Indiana, with a release date of October 26, 2033. He was arrested, tried, and sentenced to twenty-six years on vague conspiracy charges.

The federal government became interested in Schaeffer when he began giving public speeches that taught liberty and denounced corruption in the government. He was a visionary and a movement leader. He not only identified the problems within the government; he took the initiative to correct these problems.

Schaeffer ran for the Alaska House of Representatives in 2008 and was the Alaskan delegate for the Continental Congress in 2009. He started the Second Amendment Task Force, Peacekeepers Militia, and Liberty Bell system in Fairbanks, Alaska. He taught others how to build these community supports in their hometowns across the country.

Government officials became concerned and took action to silence Schaeffer. The Federal Bureau of Investigation (FBI) sent in agent provocateurs to spy on Schaeffer and attempted to get him to agree to commit an act of violence for which they could arrest him.

Schaeffer never did agree to their plan, but he was still sentenced for conspiracy to kill federal agents. They accomplished this by not allowing evidence to be brought before the jury that would have proved him innocent. The court also did not explain to the jury what was required to convict on conspiracy charges. The uninformed jury ruled with a guilty verdict.

During the first five years of Schaeffer's imprisonment, he wrote poetry and lyrics as a way to mourn his loss of freedom and separation from his wife and two young children. These lyrics were feared to have been lost within the prison after Schaeffer was thrown into solitary confinement and placed at CMU in the fall of 2016. They have been recovered and are now available to the public.

Man Against Man

These are the 24-point, Maoist, psych-warfare methods currently used in the black site CMU prison where Schaeffer Cox is held. It is infamously known as "The Asklepieion Program," and it is illegal under numerous international human rights treaties. The physical torture methods are kept far more secret. Former CMU prisoners and guards have confirmed their existence but refused to elaborate.

1. Physical removal of prisoners to areas sufficiently isolated to effectively break or seriously weaken close emotional ties.

2. Segregation of all natural leaders.

3. Use of cooperative prisoners as leaders.

4. Prohibition of group activities not in line with the brainwashing objectives.

5. Spying on the prisoners and reporting back private material.

6. Tricking men into written statements which are then shown to others.

7. Exploitation of opportunists and informers.

8. Convincing the prisoners that they can trust no one.

9. Treating those who are willing to collaborate in far more lenient ways than those who are not.

10. Punishing those who show uncooperative attitudes.

11. Systematic withholding of mail.

12. Preventing contact with anyone nonsympathetic to the method of treatment and regimen of the captive populace.

13. Building a group conviction among the prisoners that they have been abandoned by and totally isolated from the social order.

14. Disorganization of all group standards among the prisoners.

15. Undermining of all emotional supports.

16. Preventing prisoners from writing home or to friends in the community regarding the conditions of their confinement.

17. Making available and permitting access to only those publications and books that contain materials which are neutral to or supportive of the desired new attitudes.

18. Placing individuals into new ambiguous situations for which the standards are kept deliberately unclear and then putting pressure on them to conform to what is desired in order to win favor and reprieve from the pressure.

19. Placing individuals whose willpower has been severely weakened or eroded into a living situation with several others who are more advanced in their thought reform and whose job it is to further the undermining of the individuals' emotional supports which were begun by isolating them from family and friends.

20. Using techniques of character invalidation, e.g., humiliations, revilement, shouting to induce feelings of guilt, fear and suggestibility, coupled with sleeplessness, an exacting prison regimen and periodic interrogational interviews.

21. Meeting all insincere attempts to comply with cellmates' pressures with renewed hostility.

22. Repeated pointing out to prisoner by cellmates of where he was in the past, or is in the present, not even living up to his own standards or values.

23. Rewarding of submission and subservience to the attitudes encompassing the brainwashing objectives with a lifting of pressure and acceptance as a human being.

24. Providing social emotional supports which reinforce the new attitudes.

—List of 24 methods from Edward Schein, "Man Against Man," presentation to the Federal Bureaus of Prisons Systems, Washington, DC, 1961, as found in *Let Freedom Ring: A Collection of Documents from the Movements to Free U.S. Political Prisoners,* edited by Matt Meyer (Oakland, California: PM Press, 2008), 73–74. See also the pamphlet titled *Breaking Men's Minds* about behavior control in Marion, Illinois.

Contents

Not Quite Lost

by Schaeffer Cox

Verse 1

It seems like it's gone but it's all around

It hides because it's shy

It's not quite lost and not quite found

I heard it once it made me cry

(Chorus)

You'll know it when you come across it

It's never gone for long

Don't believe it if they say we lost it

Sometimes little things are strong

Verse 2

There was a boy who had it until he lost it at school

It's used up so fast on a crowd

He learned so much and still turned out a fool

Can't hear quiet in a world turned up so loud

Verse 3

There was a girl who made it though she started late

Put it in the food she fed her family

She may just change the world with a pinch on every plate

Burn a little candle for humanity

Not Quite Lost, continued

Verse 4

There was a man who killed it working day and night

He would find it anywhere it hides

But the thing he killed was in him I guess he saw the light

Felt his true allegiance now he's changing sides

Verse 5

A happy couple found it screaming in the sheets

Spicy little secrets fun to keep

Church and state is not invited when man and woman meets

Wrap an arm around her, hold her while she sleeps

Verse 6

There was a little baby who gave it to his mother

It made her blossom like a flower

She gave it back to her son who grew up and gave it to another

It flooded all the world and drowned the Ivory Tower

Verse 7

There was a cruel banker who said its time on earth was over

He made machines to change our nature

He got drunk on power but the common man was sober

He rewrote the past but couldn't write the future

Not Quite Lost, continued

Verse 8

I picked a wildflower with my finger and my thumb

Looked into a big blue sky

I brought it to my nose and smelled the smell of what's to come

This will live forever even if I die

A Lion's Heart

by Schaeffer Cox

Verse 1

A man in his home who is ready to die

His family has gathered to tell him goodbye

Takes his son by the hand and tells him he's proud

Then he slips from this life and he's wrapped in a shroud

(Chorus)

And a man with a lion's heart

Knows how to live and he knows how to die

And a man with a lion's heart

Knows how to fight and he knows how to cry

He's a man with a lion's heart

He's a man with a lion's heart

Verse 2

A man torn to pieces 'cause he stood for what's right

Buried alive in a prison where he can't see daylight

And he cries for his children he won't see as they grow

But a conscience that's clear makes his darkened cell glow

Verse 3

He leads the charge and he suffers some blows

But the cost of the battle taught him all that he knows

So he stores up his knowledge for the day of its need

And he's won half the battle because his mind has been freed

A Lion's Heart, continued

Verse 4

A baby is born, learns to be brave from his dad
He'll change the world later, for now he's a lad
But a day is soon coming that he'll live with no fear
Lift his voice like a banner that the people can hear

Verse 5

There's a season of life when you go off to war
And there's a season of life when you don't fight any more
And he knows them apart because he did them both well
And he still has his pride because he never would sell

Hope of a Better Past

by Schaeffer Cox

Verse 1

It appears to me that you're moving on
What any woman ought to do
But I don't know, I could be wrong
Been awhile since I heard from you

A little more real as the years go by
Paring down my memory
Thought of you makes me wonder why
Don't know who you are to me

(Chorus)

In the end, after all, at last
Give up all hope of a better past
Let it all go and move along

Verse 2

But I can understand the awful bind you're in
So I don't have much to say
Things never were what they could have been
I still love you when you go away

Hope of a Better Past, continued

Sometimes I think that if I was a better man
Had seen the things I didn't see
If I hadn't panicked or had a better plan
Maybe all this didn't have to be

(Chorus)
In the end, after all, at last
Give up all hope of a better past
Let it all go and move along

Verse 3
I can let you go but there's a tie that binds
Despite the wreckage of the past
The blueberry eyes are still half mine
Even though they grow up fast

All that's left for you is to marry someone new
The husband you had has gone away
Let nature take its course, do what you gotta do
A second chance may come someday

(Chorus)
In the end, after all, at last
Give up all hope of a better past
Let it all go and move along

Hope of a Better Past, continued

Verse 4

At second glance, it can't be all that bad
To do without you in my life
You can't really lose what you never really had
You're like a sister not a wife

I can't help but wonder if your mom was right
Perhaps I'm not the man for you
I'd rather sit down in shame than stand up and fight
After all that I've been through

(Chorus)

In the end, after all, at last
Give up all hope of a better past
Let it all go and move along

Verse 5

You grow up under her protecting arms
Safe and sound from men like me
Till I stole you away with my boyish charms
Did she see what you didn't see

Doesn't matter now it's in the past
No sense in losing heart
Some things aren't meant to last
Maybe we're better apart

Hope of a Better Past, continued

(Chorus)

In the end, after all, at last

Give up all hope of a better past

Let it all go and move along

Verse 6

The silence screams what you're too scared to say

And I can see it in your face

Can't look through the glass so you look away

Don't even bother to cut to the chase

I thought you were mine to have and to hold

That we'd make love wild and free

I guess that's just a bill of goods I was sold

Since it never came to be

(Chorus)

In the end, after all, at last

Give up all hope of a better past

Let it all go and move along

A Siren Calls

by Schaeffer Cox

Verse 1

I met you when I was a child

You wrapped me in your warmth

Your salty taste was in my mouth

No one had mastered you

They all just left you wild

A siren called my name

Verse 2

You took me from my home

You showed me foreign lands

I gave my strength to you

You took me as a boy

Returned me as a man

When a siren called my name

Verse 3

You let me ride your curves

You lay me in your sands

I dove into your depths

It took a gentle touch

From strong and fearless hands

As a siren called my name

A Siren Calls, continued

Verse 4

I saw you in a rage
It took my breath away
You were too cold to touch
But I still wanted you
So I found another way
After a siren called my name

Verse 5

Your salt runs in my veins
I taste you when I cry
My heart, it beats with you
Like rise and falling tide
You're where they'll bury me when I die
When a siren calls my name

Feather in Your Cap

by Schaeffer Cox

(Chorus)

Would my cap

Be a feather in yours

And if you shot me would you feel alright

And if I walked away right now

Would you chase me just to fight

Verse 1

Have you thought about the kids

And what this means for them

Have you thought about yourself

Of what you are and what you've been

Verse 2

Do you do anything you're told

Whether it is wrong or right

Do you think of law at all

Or do you only think of might

Verse 3

The blood of women and children

Is surely on your hands

Repent and ask forgiveness

Special Agent Sutherland

Feather in Your Cap, continued

Verse 4

Pulling the trigger or pulling the strings

You are guilty just the same

The cop on the beat or the judge on the bench

They all got someone else to blame

The Oak Tree

by Schaeffer Cox

(Chorus)

This old barn is turning gray

Twists and wilts and fades away

Return in to the ground

That it sprouted from so long ago

Before it was the old oak tree

Verse 1

Everywhere you're going

You've already been

And where you've been you'll go again

Verse 2

I had a dream

But it went away

Clouds undid my sunny day

Verse 3

The tender sprout

Will be a mighty tree

The glory lost will return to me

The future's mine like a memory

Second from the Left

by Schaeffer Cox

Verse 1

Second from the left
Is feeling light
The feeling hurts
And that's alright

Verse 2

I kept it warm
But now it's cold
Can't give it back
I'm not that bold

Verse 3

It's on a shelf
All alone
Sitting still
Like a stone

Verse 4

The feelings fade
As the weeks go by
They just do
I don't know why

Follow Me Down

by Schaeffer Cox

Follow me down
Down the road away from home
Follow me down
To a place, we've never known
Follow me down
Follow me down

Follow me down
From the place you knew before
Follow me down
From a virgin to a whore
Follow me down
Follow me down

Follow me down
To the place where I abide
Follow me down
From the tower where you hide
Follow me down
Follow me down

Follow Me Down, continued

Follow me down
To the place where lovers cry
Follow me down
Don't stop to wonder why
Follow me down
Follow me down

Follow me down
I'm so lonely since I've gone
Follow me down
I don't care if it's wrong
Follow me down
Follow me down

Follow me down
Will your hand still fit in mine
Follow me down
Let me have you one last time
Follow me down
Follow me down

Blue Dress

by Schaeffer Cox

Verse 1

A blue dress

On the floor

On a Sunday afternoon

The sunshine

On your hair

Do you realize what we're doin'

(Chorus)

We're gonna be together

Right there side by side

It's gonna last forever

'Cause you are my Martibride

Verse 2

A silver ring

With a purple stone

It's a secret

But you are my own

Verse 3

And we're so young

We don't even have a plan

But we can figure something out

We'll just keep on holding hands

Silence Tells the Truth

by Schaeffer Cox

Verse 1

December Sun

Can't tell the rising from the setting

My God I think it's done

Dreams are born and die before they've begun

(Chorus)

Love fades away like youth

Silence always tells the truth

And an hour of frozen light

Turns back to winter night

Verse 2

I sent you a picture you didn't want to see

I don't know what you want

I only know that it's not me

Seven years since I've been free

(Chorus)

Love fades away like youth

Silence always tells the truth

And an hour of frozen light

Turns back to winter night

Silence Tells the Truth, continued

Verse 3

Was it the hardened eyes

That made you turn away

Can your heart not recognize

The face of pain that tells no lies

(Chorus)

Love fades away like youth

Silence always tells the truth

And an hour of frozen light

Turns back to winter night

Verse 4

The boy you loved has died

I'm sorry for your loss

He's buried deep inside

The man from whom you now hide

(Chorus)

Love fades away like youth

Silence always tells the truth

And an hour of frozen light

Turns back to winter night

Twenty-Six Dollars

by Schaeffer Cox

Verse 1

Would you believe me if I said I was rich

Once upon a time?

That I was loved? That I loved humanity

I guess I fell on some hard times

Then some hard times fell on me

(Chorus)

Is there twenty-six dollars in your heart to

Help a stranger?

If you look into my eyes you'll see I'm

Not a danger.

Verse 2

I know I have a son, I've never met my daughter

They might be grown by now. My God I hope

It's not too late.

I'm trying to escape the chains of evil men.

I'm trying to change my fate.

Twenty-Six Dollars, continued

Verse 3

I'll walk my way to freedom, cross the mountains,

Brave the night, I'll swim the river.

Be a little more quiet and less bold.

Won't try to change the world.

Maybe I was right, but times have changed, I'm told.

Bridge

Verse 4

Pardon me Sir, do you know who I am?

I'm looking for a place that feels like home

Where no one recognizes me.

I traveled forty days and nights to get here.

I need some distance from my memories.

Verse 5

Expect a wave of broke down men like me.

Truth and justice both are going out of style.

I might need to be quiet for a while.

Got strung up for a show they called a trial, they tied and dragged me for a mile.

If I can get away from here I can learn again to smile.

Who I Am

by Schaeffer Cox

You can't take my soul
'Cause free is who I am
Put my body in a cage
But you just have half my man
And a better day is coming
When Babylon is gone
And the king will ride again
Upon his pale steed
My bones and soul united
At last they both are freed
So guide me safely till your coming
Around these statutes born of sin
And the system of injustice
Made by wicked men
Your righteous law is simple
From beginning to the end
If you hurt someone, restore them
And then begin again

Daybreak

by Schaeffer Cox

Verse 1

Trumpet blows

Thunder peals

Dust settles

And reveals

(Chorus)

As my soul is breaking

The day is breaking too

As my soul is breaking

The day is breaking too

Verse 2

The prisoner and

The dead are loose

The victims of the

Corrupt noose

SET FREE

Verse 3

A new day dawns

A trumpet songs

I'm marching in the

Company of the KING

Daybreak, continued

Verse 4

I recollect the darkened day

The pain is gone, the strength has stayed

My soul was in a furnace made for thee

Turn the Page

by Schaeffer Cox

Verse 1

High into the mountains is where I will go

High above all the fighting below

(Chorus)

Above your petty rage

Above your human cage

You wrote your chapter

Now let me turn the page

Verse 2

Love the ones who grovel at your feet

But loathe the day that you and I should meet

That's the day when you will taste defeat.

Verse 3

The orphans you made will be orphans no more

A river of blood will settle the score

And a sentry will stand at your door

Verse 4

Love is made to conquer hate

Love topples pretended state

And all are subject to fate

Strange Desire

by Schaeffer Cox

I'm gonna laugh when I shouldn't laugh
I'm gonna look when you say to look away
Not gonna keep my hands to myself
Not gonna watch while others play

Don't want to be your dried-up Marigold
Lying on the path where you walk by
I can't feed your strange desire
To watch me shrivel up and die

I don't know how they made you think this way
They chased your nature underground
I don't know why you thought it would be ok
To shun the happy things we found

I'm going back to find that waterfall
The bed of moss where I got laid
I'm gonna find the fairy in that hotel room
This time I won't be afraid

I'm gonna find that brand new flame
And let her take my breath away
I'm not gonna hide a single one of my thoughts
Or worry about what I say

27

Noon to Midnight

by Schaeffer Cox

Verse 1

Midnight every night

The memory of you comes

I struggle and I fight

Verse 2

My mind has moved on

I know it's all over for us

But my heart's still hanging on

Verse 3

I'm well composed all day

I leave you in the past

Sleep lets out the demons held at bay

Verse 4

I read the words inside my wedding band

Put it on and take it off again

This isn't what we planned

Verse 5

I guess you moved on too

Left the past behind

What else could you do?

Noon to Midnight, continued

Verse 6

A message comes each day at noon

When they never call my name

Maybe I'll stop hoping soon

Verse 7

She doesn't smile, she doesn't weep

Maybe she still loves me

But that's a secret she will keep

Don't Look Down

by Schaeffer Cox

Verse 1

Here it comes!

Get your ass off the fence!

Find your balls!

Get a little confidence!

She's about to blow!

History's calling for you on the stage.

It finally hit the fan!

Here comes one hundred years of pent up rage.

(Chorus)

Don't look down!

Ride the lightning bolt you found

Don't look down!

Don't look down!

Don't look down!

Verse 2

We've heard it all

The time for talk is past!

People have had enough!

The world's aflame and burning fast

Don't Look Down, continued

Finish it now, take your chance!
Nobody's gonna make it to round two!
Help ain't coming, Dummy!
Just take it! It belongs to you!

Verse 3

Taste it once, you're hooked for life
It's easier than you thought
You're your own damn boss
Shed the bullshit you were taught

A few survive but none alive
You've got nothing left to lose!
Die in chains or righteous rage
Don't you have a point to prove?

Verse 4

It doesn't matter either way
If they kill you, if you win
They lost a slave today
Take 'em somewhere that they've never been!

Teach them so they won't forget
Just try to own the human race
Take a gamble with your life!
The last thing you see will be my face!

31

Don't Look Down, continued

Verse 5

You think you have a master plan?
Screw you and all your bankster friends!
You're gonna need a deeper cave!
The dying starts when life begins

Smell that sweat that's on your neck?
I love that smell, that smell of fear
Your shifty eyes give you away
Hold your breath. Your end is near

Give Yourself to Me

by Schaeffer Cox

Hello, I've waited years for you

Now cast your spell on me

Show me, how you want it to be

Let's see those long and magic legs

Your tongue can lick away my chains

Your smell takes away the memory of the cage

To feel you melting in my hands

I'm back, I'm a man again

Taste the fountain of youth

The one you open up to me

Erase the years I lost

Remind me that I'm free

Give yourself to me

Promised Land

by Schaeffer Cox

(Chorus)

My lover

Has been ripped away

But I know I'll see her

Again someday

Violent men

Are all around

I want a friend who is faithful

But none can be found

Verse 1

I wring my hands

What can I do?

It kills me to watch

What they're doing to you

Verse 2

My baby boy

Asks why I am gone

Why I can't come home

If I've done nothing wrong

Promised Land, continued

Verse 3

The sound of your voice

Is gentle and strong

I know you can't keep going

If this goes on for long

Verse 4

Abba save me

Out of their hand

Bless me and lead me

To your promised land

Raindrops

by Schaeffer Cox

Verse 1

Every little stream is rising, feel the rain coming down
Water ripples around the stones
It's not enough to cut a path
Or take me to where I'm goin'

(Chorus)

The sun is going down, on who I used to be
It doesn't hurt like it did before
I couldn't care even if I tried
It has to be buried if it has died

Verse 2

Step in the water that trickles down the trails
Rain like tears, don't stop until the mud is clean
Takes the story to the ocean it never fills

Verse 3

Drop by drop it cuts through granite stone
Leaves a chasm in the way
Can't see the end, deepest cut I've ever known

Verse 4

Might have to go around or even form a pool
But it will get there just the same
Won't be routed by a mountain or captured by a fool

Man and a Wire
by Schaeffer Cox

Man wearing a wire trying to bust me
I said, Hey friend, is that who you want to be?
Tell the truth, how'd they get you?
Is it something you did?

You steal a car, rob a house,
Buy some weed from the wrong kid?

Police sit you down, tell you who you talked to,
Everywhere that you've been?
They'd been watching you
Made you confess all of your sins.
Did they scare you? Make you work for them?

Tape a wire over your sad heart.
Tomorrow morning's when the work starts.
Did they say they had the power to forgive you?
Did you take the time to think that claim through?

You didn't hurt them. Who can let you off the hook?
Not the cops, but the dude whose car you took.

Crooked cops don't need help from you.
Go ahead, you know what to do
Just do the right thing bro, I'll forgive you
Honor shouldn't have a price
C'mon cops, you better think twice

Cave in to Love

by Schaeffer Cox

Burn with passion for the wild things
Feel the joy that a child brings

Cave in to love, lay down your pride
Forgive again on the other side

The height of life when two are one
For all that's right a victory won.

Won't Be Forever

by Schaeffer Cox

(Chorus)

This

This won't be

This

This won't be

Forever

Verse 1

Like rain that goes away

Or the winter with no day

Verse 2

Like fire burning gold

Joseph who got sold

Verse 3

Like the wait to wed your bride

Like the rocks beneath the tide

Verse 4

You'll awaken from this dream to find

God's restored you all the time

They robbed from you, your children and your wife

Won't Be Forever, continued

Verse 5

At last their fate is sealed

At last your wounds are healed

It's the first day of the best days of your life

Run with Me
by Schaeffer Cox

Verse 1

I've cried enough tears
In the time we've been apart
To grow a garden full of roses for you

(Chorus)

The wait is over
Our world is crumbled at our feet but I am yours
Run with me. . . . Forever and ever and ever and ever
Says the ring, you gave me long ago
I'm yours again

Verse 2

To hold your hands
And gaze into your eyes
I see the soul that saw me through

Verse 3

I feel your breath
A breath of life that makes me warm
Our bodies are woven together like our soul

Verse 4

You're the cradle of life
You made our house a home
I'm so in love with you

Hatin' You a Little Less

by Schaeffer Cox

Verse 1

Been three years since you cut and run

I had to learn to love all over again

I'd forgotten how to have fun

(Chorus)

Well it sorta snuck up on me baby

But it is what it is, I guess

Lately I been hatin' you a little less

Verse 2

I'm not saying I could be yours again

There's a lot of space between us

But we're a little closer to lovers if we're friends

Verse 3

Can't predict the future or forget the past

Let go the wheel, car just spins

Can't change a thing when we're going this fast

Three Promises to Keep

by Schaeffer Cox

(Spoken)

Been down for a long time now

Got to get back on my feet

Travelin' light these days

Got nothing but three promises to keep

I want to feel the sun on my neck, while I plant a tree

I want to swim in the ocean, the only place that I feel free

I want to sit by a fire, just big enough for me

Dirt under my nails

A baby tree in a cup

I feel alive again

My own grave's been dug up

Rise and fall with the swell

As I swim out from shore

Wash out all the thoughts

I don't need any more

The tangled wood that's burning

Casts a glow on this beach

So I snuggle with the flicker

Just out of darkness reach

More Is Not Enough

by Schaeffer Cox

Verse 1

Across the room I saw his eyes

That's when I knew he was the one

That's when I knew I was his wife

I didn't make it known at first

I held my tongue and feared the worst

I felt like I'd known him all my life

(Chorus)

My mother says he's just a boy

That I'm too young to know

There's an ugly side of love

But there's a magic in this joy

And when we touch it makes me glow

One sip and more is not enough

Verse 2

When worlds . . . collide

Oh, and stars come crashing down

Down to this fallen ground

You feel those sparkles everywhere

Young love is in the air

More Is Not Enough, continued

Verse 3

Our passion burning in a rage
We loosed a tiger from its cage
Young lovers melted into one

Am I a sinner and a slut
Flaunt myself and pay the price
We did it more than once
We did it more than twice

Verdict

by Schaeffer Cox

Verse 1

My life is ripped away

The boy that needs me oh so bad

24 guilty eyes looked away

I am led away in chains

Scream to the father that I love

Can my son make it on his own

With no father in his home?

(Chorus)

How can this be?

Oh my God!

My God, how can this be?

Verse 2

A wicked liar has his way

I'm numb, face down on the floor

Stunning disbelief I'm a man

Who's never going home

And all I tried to do was right

How in 12 not even one could see?

Is a verdict from a man? Did it have to be?

Verdict, continued

Verse 3

My Son, oh my God, my Son

To grow up without me

My Son, my Son, innocent and sweet

God! My God, oh God

Can this be? Oh God, my Son

My Son, oh God, my Son

Crazy One

by Schaeffer Cox

Verse 1

An endless string of identical days

The best opinions are homemade

My life's a living haze

(Chorus)

I can tell you why I've done

What I have done

Am I still the crazy one?

Verse 2

Colang don't have to let me see my boy

The fiddler knows the truth

The brute will try to rob your joy

Verse 3

Go around in circles like the razor wire

I don't play cards or get in fights

Bite your tongue, quench the fire

Verse 4

Kites and bendels and chesters, now I know

The very minute I'll let it go

Trick bag, get a sack, keester all the dope

Crazy One, continued

Verse 5

To see your kids throw someone under the bus

PC up the prison bitch

If you help us lie you'll be free like us

Verse 6

Sneaky, sneaky, one guy in four vans

Just put me in my cage

Run, run around town, got secret plans

Hurt Feelings

by Schaeffer Cox

Verse 1

It hurt my feelings

When I heard them talk about me that way

I'm just a gentle man

Never thought I'd be a terrorist someday

And here I am, but I wouldn't be the man

They wanted me to be

I stood alone, I wouldn't give in

But they still want'a lock me up

And throw away the key

(Chorus)

It hurts my feelings

That everyone's scared of me

It hurts my feelings

That my kids don't have a daddy

It hurts my feelings

When you point your finger at me

When I gave up everything for you.

Hurt Feelings, continued

Verse 2

It makes me cry

That you broke into my home with all your friends

Threw the babies on the ground

And made their mothers cry

After we showed you love

We refused to do you harm

You still attacked the women and the kids

And you leave me asking why

Verse 3

You took my home and you ruined my name

You paid a million dollars to have me framed

You even tried to kill me and another man

You want to orphan my kids and widow my wife

But I can still forgive you just the same

Just stop right now, we can still be friends

I have loved you all along

Everything

by Schaeffer Cox

Verse 1

We took off into outer space

Like a cosmic turtle in a cosmic race

(Chorus)

We lost everything we ha-aad

But we had everything we didn't lo-oose

'Cause when it's time to leave your cloak

There ain't time for you to choose

Verse 2

A couple bags and a wad of cash

How far ya get depends on the price of gas

Verse 3

There's a time to flee when the wicked attack

You walk away and you don't look back

Verse 4

They stole my fortune and they took my home

But I'm ok as long as I can roam

Verse 5

My little girl and my little boy

And my gentle wife are my joy

Everything, continued

Verse 6

All in all, it hasn't been that bad

The ups and down shouldn't make you sad

Verse 7

He gives it all and he takes away

Just open your hand, it'll be ok

Good Times

by Schaeffer Cox

I didn't hurt a soul

I didn't do a damn thing wrong

But I'm here lying in the cold

Nothing to warm me but this song

I just want to be free

Having good times with my friends

This ain't the way it's meant to be

But it ain't the way the story ends

So I'll just sing to get me through

I'll just sing to get me to the other side

I'll just sing to soothe the pain

I'll just sing to pass the time

I'll just sing because I can

I'll just sing to help me cope

I will sing because there is hope

Gentle Power

by Schaeffer Cox

Verse 1

Through a pane of glass

In chains, I tell him stories

I smile and cry

His heart knows something's wrong

He asks me if those men are hurting me

I tell him that I won't be here for long

(Chorus)

By gentle powers lovingly surrounded

Afflicted much but still my soul is not dismayed

Abiding in your provision of the moment

Your wisdom and your grace let come what may

Verse 2

I render unto CZAR what is CZAR's

But won't bend the knee to any one

The sorrow of my young son reveals

That every generation pays the price

Verse 3

The innocent afflicted by the wicked

Not only me but also my wife who bears alone . . .

Who bears alone the burden of this strife.

Have Your Way

by Schaeffer Cox

Verse 1

I cried like grown men do

When I remember her face

I forgot this place

(Chorus)

You can have your way

You can have your way

You can have your way

I don't even care about you anymore

Verse 2

My family fell down when the music played

They are easy to deceive

They want their world of make-believe

Verse 3

Violence on the innocent, my hands are bound

I'm a gladiator in a cage

Mortal combat with my rage

Verse 4

The life I knew evaporates and floats away

Every day's the same to me

An endless string of misery

Have Your Way, continued

Verse 5

The honest and courageous men sit in chains

The brazen liars laugh out loud

The violent badge is somehow proud

The Soil That I Loved

by Schaeffer Cox

Verse 1

I don't have anything to say

That I haven't said before

I'm all out of precious gems

For you to ignore

(Chorus)

I'll go my way alone and won't look back

I tried hard and I meant well but they thought

It was a joke

I spilled my blood and tears and treasure

For the soil that I loved and I was all alone

Turns out this land I'm fight'n for cannot

Be my home

No one wants to see it now, the picture

Will be clearer when they're looking through the smoke

Verse 2

I've said my peace and made my stand

Now I'm mov'n on

You can beat and kill the speaking man

But the words will still live on

The Soil That I Loved, continued

Verse 3

I guess that its ok to keep the secrets
That I know
When all the people want is to believe
The show

Cheery Poison

by Schaeffer Cox

Verse 1

Don't know when it started
Or how it's gonna end
Lots of people talking to me
Maybe snitches, maybe friends

(Chorus)

I'm not wanted where I live
So I run far and wide
To find a place I can live
Where I can think what I want
And speak what I think
And I don't have to hide

Verse 2

I threw a fortune to the wind and
Walked away to show the cops some grace
Then they beat my family down and stuck
A rifle in their face.

Verse 3

Your lies are cheery poison
The people lick it from your hand
But I'm no competition
The truth's not in demand

The Far Bank

by Schaeffer Cox

Verse 1

I've crossed a lot of rivers deep and far

And every one I come to is colder than the last

(Chorus)

On the other side

On the far bank

Meet me on the far bank

On the far bank's where I'll be

On the far bank

On the far bank

In the end is where I'll be

Verse 2

I've traveled a long, long, way alone

He can't turn back who doesn't have a home

Verse 3

People try to kill me so I have to stay away

I'll just keep on drift'n till I see the King someday

Verse 4

The difference in a peasant and a prince is hard to see

The one is living scared and the other one is free

The Far Bank, continued

Verse 5

The freezing current ripples o'er my brow
Each man has a time to cross. I guess my time is now

One and the Same

by Schaeffer Cox

Smoking buildings, masses cower
Stolen loot to build your tower

Broken men don't need a wall
In secret, you're behind it all

Stare into the mirror of your enemy's face
Point, scream blame and shame

Dim the lights, work the crowd, play the game
Never mind you're one and the same

There's a point to all these pointless rules
Good men kiss the feet of fools

Submission absolves you of all your sins
By evil ways come evil ends

Not all men are judged the same
You can do no wrong if you're in the gang

The narco-lobby rides again
Black robes cover all their sin

One and the Same, continued

Five years old a judge's whore
Broken life left on the floor

Embarrassment is all he fears
He gave me twenty-seven years

Flash your badge and hypnotize
Control the people with your lies

Be Okay

by Schaeffer Cox

It's gonna be okay!
Best things in the world don't change

Be a strong man, get a hot wife
Live fearless, have a good life
Best things in the world don't change

Sexy bridesmaid, marry the best man
Take your breath away, take your man's hand
Best things in the world don't change

Who teaches babies how to smile?
Who says kids are gon' outta style
Best things in the world don't change

A job well done, by a father
Teaching a trade to his first son
Best things in the world don't change

People are good, except for a few
Try'n to say humanity is through
Best things in the world don't change

65

Be Okay, continued

Starve the bastards out in their ivory tower
Happy people have our own power
Best things in the world don't change

Nature's gonna have her way, we gonna be okay
Gonna be a new day, IT'S GON' OUR WAY!

Final Voyage

by Schaeffer Cox

Verse 1

She's wood and brass, mast, a deck and sails

We've been aground, through wind and wave and fire

But she's still here with the scars that tell her tales

The tide is slowly falling, I see ripples on the reef

I row to shore, turn my back on the future

You start to list, I just look on in disbelief

(Chorus)

I'm not a captain without you

And what are you without me at your helm?

But we've made our final voyage on the sea

I'm leaving you, you're leaving me

Verse 2

The water's clear and cold, I start to see the ground

It's raising from the depths to meet me

A new home to which I'm bound

From shore I see your pennants waving in the breeze

It hurts to look, it hurts to look away

My soul is in your keel, I stumble to my knees

Final Voyage, continued

Verse 3

Before you're gone I turn and walk away

I want to remember you as you were

In my memory, on the waves is where you'll stay

Full and by the wind with a following sea

Your ghost will haunt the waves of our beloved sea

I'll think of you and you will think of me

Knowledge with Intent

by Schaeffer Cox

(Chorus)

Don't look behind the curtain

Think twice about that itch

Beware what you may find there

The truth's an ugly bitch

Verse 1

See the truth, it will make you pale

Nothing left is sacred, everything's for sale

Verse 2

Throw your ass in prison, 'cause of what you believe

They got the press in'er pocket, gonna help'm deceive

Verse 3

Once you know what you're not supposed to know

Do-si-do, down you go, sitt'n in the hoosegow

Verse 4

You won't believe the shit I've been through

For knowledge with intent to distribute

Sundown

by Schaeffer Cox

Verse 1

He came to tell me things while I'm still sleeping

He comes to tell me things I need to know

I hate the noise, my mind is racing

But I can hear the words when thought are slow

(Chorus)

Hold your breath until the sun goes down

Until the waking nightmare fades

Hold your breath until the sun goes down

Your real life on the screen is played

Hold your breath until the sun goes down

Hold your breath until the sun goes down

Verse 2

I toss and turn upon my bed

The worries of the day are brought to life

The thing I love escaping from my head

As for a moment, I can see my son and wife

Verse 3

My troubled heart cries out HAAAA

It's silent screaming seems to fill the air

No end in sight, the children suffer

The passive pain of having no one there

Sundown, continued

Verse 4

If you have a promise it will keep you through the night

The man who keeps his promise can live through any fight

A promise can sustain you

Invigorate or tame you

Verse 5

The powers can't abide you

The ignorant will chide you

But in your heart, you'll know all is right

You've the promise of tomorrow for tonight

My Only Dollar

by Schaeffer Cox

If I had a dollar
From everyone
Who promised they'd be by my side

And if I paid a dollar
For everyone
Who got scared and ran to hide

I would have one lonely dollar
And you'd be standing by my side

I'd close my eyes
And I'd take your hand
I'm glad you love me
I'm glad you understand

A million dollars
Came and went away
You're my only dollar
And everything's okay
I've got one dollar
I've got one dollar
I've got one dollar
I've got one lonely dollar to my name

Bury Me at Sea

by Schaeffer Cox

Turns out it's not as bad as I thought it would be
Death Angels come a callin'. They're here to rescue me

A shank under my ribs is planted like a seed
From the bureaucratic slow death, I have now been freed

His arm is wrapped around me, I stare into his face
These moments while I'm fading I've come back to the human race

No more chasing shadows, no more can they tell me no
No more pretend justice, now they can't use me for their show

Don't let them keep my body. Please bury me at sea
I only want red roses thrown by friends and family

The things I dreaded losing, I lost them long ago
Tell my children I'll be with them wherever they may go

When the storm is gone, bury me at sea
When the storm is gone, bury me at sea
When the waves are calm
When the waves are calm
Bury me at sea
Bury me at sea
At sea. At sea

Don't Know What Else to Do

by Schaeffer Cox

It's been about a year or maybe it's been more like four,
I'm still not over you

Everything is settled, I still can't decide
What parts of love are living, what parts of love has died

I wish I had done better, I know how I'm to blame
But something big was missing, I can't go back to things being the
same

Some of it's forever, and some's forever gone
I hate you and I love enough to want you to move on

I don't know how I'll take it when you get another man.
You're smart and fun and pretty. If you want to you can

I'd like to find a new girl, if I ever get a chance.
One who doesn't know what I've been through who'll
Just smile and hold my hand.

But if she's going to love me she'll have to love you too.
'Cause I'll love you forever, I don't know what else to do.

Run . . . with Me Forever

by Schaeffer Cox

Verse 1

You, you think you know what's good

A man, to do things you never could

He looks alright from a distance

A hero, fighting in the resistance

You, you didn't know what to say

Didn't have the nerve to look, or to look away

(Chorus)

Who needs a plan?

Follow your heart

And just take my hand!

Run with me faster and faster

Run through the night

Two steps ahead of disaster

Swallow the fear, never say never

Run, run with me forever

Verse 2

You said I do, and you changed your name

Too young to leave home, too old to live on a chain

Overnight you were free, independent, and wealthy

Had to grow up and cut your ties to be healthy

But Mom had to keep her hooks in your skin

Said you were wayward, said your love was a sin

Run . . . with Me Forever, continued

(Chorus)

Verse 3

You start to think twice, about the man that you marry
To live a life without fear, is a little bit scary
You have second thoughts about life in the saddle
Running from the law and running to battle
A robe with no soul mounts a major attack
She runs away, I stand and fight back

(Chorus)

Verse 4

She fell for me 'cause I was wild and sexy
But she needs a man who is tame, to just be her besty
There's only so much pain, danger, and scandal
That a good girl like her can handle
It's been a few years since I've heard her voice
She didn't say so but I hear the choice

(Chorus)

Run . . . with Me Forever, continued

Verse 5

It's a big scary world but I'll go it alone

Breakneck speed into the unknown

I'm sure there's a girl who's been where I've been

Who doesn't fear danger, or the taste of skin

If I can win this battle I'll begin again

If I can win this battle I'll begin again

I'll begin again

Begin again

Again

Not the Man for You

by Schaeffer Cox

Verse 1

Looking back on all our years

Didn't hear a voice of thunder

That made me question what is real

It's the little things that make me wonder

(Chorus)

Maybe I'm just not the man for you

Maybe I'm just not the man for you

Maybe I'm just not the man for you

Anymore

Verse 2

To tell the truth it used to make me cry

That nothing ever seemed to fit

But still I loved you in a certain way

Too much to give up or to quit

Verse 3

Can a thing be forced when it isn't there?

In this place where passion doesn't grow?

Somewhere out there there's an answer

The answer that I'll never know

Not the Man for You, continued

Verse 4

Can we be friends though the fire didn't catch?

I wanted it all but I'll settle for part

I can find a girl where the passion is strong

You can keep my hand but I need my heart

Let the Future Go

by Schaeffer Cox

Verse 1

I didn't used to be this way

But then the curtains all fell down

Am I better for the ugly truth I found?

Verse 2

Can't give back what you gave to me

Can't go back to thinking that I'm free

I looked up the skirt and had to pay

Verse 3

A phone call 15 minutes on Wednesday

Do you love me like you did before?

I understand and if you can't take it anymore

Verse 4

Silence ringing in my empty ears

Survived the fire but can't survive the years

It's dead but I don't want to throw it away

Verse 5

Broken pieces scattered on the ground

Get picked up and put in something new

If I was there that's what I would do

Let the Future Go, continued

Verse 6

You still haunt my dreams at night

No love but no reason to fight

You're just there like echoes of a sound

Verse 7

The man you knew died a long, long, time ago

Stone cold can't be brought back to life

Don't think this one's cut out for a wife

Verse 8

Drafted into a solitary trade

To meet him now you'd probably be afraid

Keep your memories in a box but let the future go.

It Pains My Soul

by Schaeffer Cox

Verse 1

It doesn't matter what it means

I must be what I must be

Can't fight against the truth

Can't lie about what I see

(Chorus)

And it pains my soul (repeat three times)

That we ended up this way

Verse 2

They put a high price

On speech that's free

There's a mean ol' lesson

They want-ta teach me

Verse 3

The violence of the man

Isn't hard to understand

Like the scared and foolish people

That are eating from its hand

It Pains My Soul, continued

Verse 4

It's all they have ever known
It's all they'll ever be
The man who's born a slave
Has no longing to be free

Verse 5

Oh! And Americans are easy
Far too easy to deceive
All they have to do is tell them
Lies that they want to believe

I Used to Be Nice

by Schaeffer Cox

If I had stayed, just a face in the crowd
If I hadn't spoken, hadn't been so loud

If I had kept going, like I didn't see
If I'd said nothing, would they have picked me?

For this hell, where grown men cry
Where thought is forbidden, and futures die

I had a name, but they took it back
I did the right thing, got stabbed in the back

I used to be nice, but now I am mean
There aren't any words, for things I have seen

I went from a man, to just a cog on the wheel
From learning to love, to learning not to feel

Wake up at night, need some revenge
They take an innocent life, and don't even cringe

Life in the hole, no windows, no door, no light of day
Just one of six million, wasting away.

Consider This
by Schaeffer Cox

(Chorus)
Consider this, consider this my friends
Consider all you've ever know
Everything you thought was right
Consider this, consider this

Verse 1
My parents are orphans of the state
They're in love with everything I hate
I know you follow God
But do you think it's rather odd
To have Satan as a sitter while you wait?

Verse 2
It's the highest honor that I can receive
To be thrown in prison because of what I believe
TV and secret police
Is all it takes to fleece
The Americans, they're easy to deceive

Verse 3
They're only playing dress up and pretend
Just look at all the trouble that we're in
You think your Congress is divine
And they might be in your mind
But in the end, they're only fallen men

Beyond the Darkness

by Schaeffer Cox

I've been beyond the darkness
I've wrestled with the dragon
It's not that bad, my friend
But worse than you'd imagine

Some thrive, some die, some disappear, but none remain the same
From blood to sweat to salty tears for glory and for shame

I'm where you are going
Your life's a spinning dime
Both the sides are tails
And you don't have much time

The State devours innocence
Like fire burns through straw
Your dream world is burning
Awake and stand in awe

I'll Be a God

by Schaeffer Cox

We finance the rise
And we finance the fall
The losers will die
And the winners take all
But winners will lose when their debt is recalled

They call it a victory
They'll have a parade
But the debt that we give them
Cannot be repaid
'Cause they owe us more than dollars
Than have ever been made

I used to feel bad
Because it's so cruel
But people this dumb
Deserve to be fooled
We're kings of a world that begs to be ruled

Soon I'll be a god
And you will be too
We'll kill the whole world
Keep only a few
We'll merge with machines when humanity's through

Justice & Hope—Fear & Lies
by Schaeffer Cox

Verse 1

I know it made them scared
I can understand
The keeper of the slaves
Confronted by a man
The coward in his heart
Plots his evil plan
Snuff out every light
With his wicked hand

(Chorus)

Where has justice gone?
Will I see hope again?
Is this place I'm going
Worse than where I've been?
Can I have a home
Where truth is not a sin?

Verse 2

You came before the dawn
Machine guns in the night
A mask to hide your face
You knew it wasn't right
The women and the kids
Didn't even fight
A child's life destroyed
Before the sun's first light

Justice & Hope—Fear & Lies, continued

(Chorus)

Verse 3

The magician called a judge

Spins his web of lies

I see the truth he hides

Behind his beady eyes

I reject the stories

Told by all the spies

He'll never break my will

No matter how he tries

(Chorus)

Your Only Friend
by Schaeffer Cox

Verse 1

There's a time, people listening

There's a time, no one is around

There's a time, people hate you

Talk you up and then they throw you down

(Chorus)

Among the faithful? Am I among the few?

Will I be able to do what no one else was willing to do?

They'll throw rocks in the beginning

And they'll throw roses in the end

The crowds will ebb and flow

The crowds will ebb and flow

Your conscience is your only friend

Verse 2

But there's a few who are faithful

Bravery that will make you cry

Good men keep on giving

First to live may be the first to die

Verse 3

Average folks, average men

Crowds are scarce when the odds are grim

There's a road where no one else has been

Hate you now, and love you in the end

I Don't Believe in You
by Schaeffer Cox

Verse 1

I don't believe in rich
I don't believe in poor
I don't believe in virgins
I don't believe in whores

You're all the same to me
You lost me at hello

Verse 2

I don't believe in church
I don't believe in state
I don't believe in charity
I don't believe in hate

Sell it to yourself
I don't want your wares

Verse 3

I don't believe in judge
I don't believe in cop
I don't believe in bottom
I don't believe in top

A costume black, a costume blue
Hardly an excuse

Hummingbird

by Schaeffer Cox

You think it makes a difference if you flap your little wings
But still you're at the mercy of much, much, bigger things
Just let it go! Let the ground go screaming by!

Don't know where I'm go'n
Don't know where I've been
If this wind keeps on blow'n
I'll probably circle 'round again
Just a hummingbird in this hurricane

Don't ask me what happened or if I have a plan
For sure the one who's lying will say he understands
Just let it go! We don't need the reasons why!

A little streak of gladness in the storm of hurt
Children have to grow up, and grown-ups turn to dirt
Just let it go! It's okay to let 'em cry!

The Ballad of Schaeffer Cox

by Schaeffer Cox

Innocence of youth and eyes of wonder
A voice that spoke like distant thunder
When I saw the smoky backroom deal
I learned the game they use to steal
Your innocence, your fortune, and your life

Come follow me we'll save the day
Expose their sins they'll run away
They're pimping kids in Ocean View
And selling snow to me and you
But once you know, you know, you can't look back

It's my heart that pulls me onward now
To stop this evil, I don't know how
But we can't lose with right on our side
They're the ones with sins to hide
So, saddle up and leave your fear, we gonna play this one by ear

In the midnight sun of two thousand ten
Is when our nightmare would begin
They came to steal our child by force
They knew we would say no, of course
We know what they do to boys his age

The Ballad of Schaeffer Cox, continued

The spies all said we must defend
Bennett said he'd join in
Fulton held us to the razor's edge
But we wouldn't take their evil pledge
We told them no and backed away

But the shadow men were on the move
Their actors had too much to lose
They'd pushed and pulled me to join their crime
But I wouldn't budge and they ran out of time
So they hatched a plot to take my life

But a soldier overheard the plan
And in that moment, he was a man
A spirit sent him to my side
If not for him I would have died
But had the danger passed for good?

I wouldn't give my only begotten son
I couldn't fight, so I had to run
A home, a life, a place to stand
I let it slip from my open hand
We turned and drove into the night

The Ballad of Schaeffer Cox, continued

Then a goon was sent to block our way
The things he did forced us to stay
He got his orders from on high
His handlers told him how to lie
He passed along the threats of death

For twenty days and twenty nights
We hid in an attic out of sight
As the handlers set their final trap
They'd shoot me dead then mount my cap
But God was with me one more time

They drove me to the execution spot
To fix "the problem," or so they thought
But the Spirit sent a second man
To disrupt their evil plan
He saved me from the instant death

I hadn't bled out in the snow
Or die with the secrets that I know
They didn't have a real plan B
But they also couldn't set me free
So, they simply buried me alive

The Ballad of Schaeffer Cox, continued

They accused me of their very sins
They told their stories to all my friends
A few believed, a few saw through
There wasn't much that I could do
My hands were bound my mouth was gagged

I watched in horror and disbelief
As I lost my life to a black-robed thief
He banned the truth and signed off on a lie
I had to watch my mother cry
As they sealed me in a living tomb

I wailed at night for the son I had lost
I knew that he would bear the cost
A sacrifice to the god of state
My heart was filled with righteous hate
For those who vandalize humanity

The daughter I loved but never knew
Who would hold her as she grew?
The wife I had but had no more
We lost the love we had before
As years upon years of silence passed

The Ballad of Schaeffer Cox, continued

But even Joseph in the days of old
Thought all was lost when he was sold
Yet he was made for bigger things
And dungeons gave us many kings
It's a fire that refines the hearts of gold

—written July 12, 2017, in "Little Gitmo" federal prison

97

I Pray on My Feet

by Schaeffer Cox

Verse 1

I remember when

We sang the song and read the book

That told us of our sin

Those were the days

When it was safe to be a man like me

Till they outlawed our ways

(Chorus)

I used to pray on my knees

But now I have to pray on my feet

It's a warrior's world now

I must be ready for the enemy's I meet

Verse 2

And there's no going back

If they have their way they'll have our heads

Unless we all attack

The future king had a few

Outlaw men who had no trace of fear

Did what they could do

I Pray on My Feet, continued

Verse 3

It's a scary sight

The softer people look away when

The men of God start to fight

My bones can hear the warrior's song

Humanity's come down to do or die

Skipped a generation but courage came back strong

We'll know how it ends before too long, the ancient warrior's song

Break the Spell

by Schaeffer Cox

Verse 1

They hang it on their walls

It's always on TV

Image in your pocket

The sun nobody sees

(Chorus)

Break the spell to get free

Break the spell to get free

If you look then you will see

Break the spell to get free

Break the spell to get free

Verse 2

The sign of giants walk among us

Leave a wake of human wreckage

Black mirrors to the future

Don't have to be the message

Verse 3

The evil eye is watching

It's an ancient superstition

To make us less than human

Is its never-ending mission

Break the Spell, continued

Verse 4

It's on every shining badge
It's on every courtroom floor
It's a poison way of thinking
We are different than before

Verse 5

The right is an illusion
It isn't even real
There's only you and me
And we never made a deal

Verse 6

Flashing rays of light
Blast in all directions
Giving make-believe permission
To their sundial erections

Verse 7

The secret priests among us
Subjugate the masses
Teach us one can own another
In their esoteric classes

Break the Spell, continued

Verse 8

We're ruled by Lucifer's religion

Secret wars, abortion stores, and prison

Sacrifice a human on the altar

Of official superstition

Verse 9

I love my country

Like a father loves a wayward son

And my heart will not stop hurting

Until this superstition's gone

Thank You from Schaeffer Cox and
His Publishers: David, Liz, and Angela

Thanks for checking out *The Lost Lyrics of Schaeffer Cox*. It warms my heart to know that someone out in the free world learned about my situation and then enjoyed the songs found inside.

I'd like to ask that you please leave a review for this book. Your honest feedback can help me craft other lyrics or books in the future that will appeal the most to my supporters. Reviews can also help others decide if this is a book that might be worthy of their time or money.

You can review the book on your favorite social media site or on Amazon.

Let's Connect!

Website

www.freeschaeffer.com

Write Letters to Schaeffer

www.freeschaeffer.com/contact

Francis Schaeffer Cox
(Note: This address does NOT accept donations.)
16179-006
FCI Terre Haute
P.O. Box 33
Terre Haute, IN 47808

NOTE: This address will change if Schaeffer is transferred to a different prison, which is common.

Visit https://www.bop.gov/inmateloc/ and search "Find By Name" using "Francis Cox."

Click on "Located at:" to find the address of the facility.

You can also search "Find By Number" and enter his Register Number of 16179-006.

To Help Schaeffer Fight for His Freedom,
Donations Are Always Accepted

1. Checks Made Out to Schaeffer Cox

Schaeffer Cox
14526 Piney Road
Mulberry, AR 72947

2. Credit Cards

https://fundrazr.com/6191Ea?ref=ab_75mvU5
https://www.paypal.me/SchaefferCox

3. Money Orders (Sent to Prison Commissary Account)

Francis Schaeffer Cox
16179-006
FBoP Lock Box
P.O. Box 474701
Des Moines, IA 50947-0001

4. Western Union Quick Pay

Francis S. Cox
16179-006
City Code: FBoP
State Code: DC

Mailing List

To be added to the postal mailing list, email your name and address to Angela at schaeffercox@gmail.com.